Glitter FM

Follow the Glitter Girls' latest adventures!
Collect all the fantastic books in the series:

Caroline Plaisted

Glitter FM

■SCHOLASTIC

Scholastic Children's Books,
Commonwealth House, 1-19 New Oxford Street,
London WC1A 1NU, UK
a division of Scholastic Ltd

London ~ New York ~ Toronto ~ Sydney ~ Auckland
Mexico City ~ New Delhi ~ Hong Kong

Published by Scholastic Ltd, 2001

ISBN 0 439 99405 5

Typeset by Falcon Oast Graphic Art Ltd
Printed by Cox & Wyman Ltd, Reading, Berks.

2 4 6 8 10 9 7 5 3 1

Chapter 1

It was Friday afternoon after school, and the Glitter Girls were getting together for a meeting at Zoe's house.

"Go on up girls," said Zoe's mum, smiling at them. "And you can take these biscuits with you too," she said, handing Meg a plate of double chocolate cookies.

"My favourite!" grinned Meg, and she shot up the stairs after Hannah, Flo and Charly, her long, wavy blonde hair swinging behind her. Sometimes, the Glitter Girls went to one of their houses straight after school to hang out. But today, they'd all gone home to change out of their school uniform and get into more comfortable stuff.

Zoe's room was the first on the right. There was a sign on the door that read KEEP OUT! GLITTER GIRLS ABOUT! Zoe had made it herself out of shiny paper and glittery ink.

Hannah knocked on the door in Glitter Girl code: RAT tat tat!

"Who's there?" hissed Zoe from the other side.

"GG!" her four friends whispered, and immediately the door was opened.

"GG" was the Glitter Girls' secret password.

Once they were inside Zoe's room, the girls all took off their jackets and piled them on the bed.

"Great T-shirt, Flo!" Hannah said, looking at her friend's cap-sleeved top. It had a pattern of groovy pink sequins on the front.

"Thanks. My mum got it for me at the weekend," Flo replied, pushing her long dark hair behind her ears.

The Glitter Girls sat in a circle on the floor and tucked into the biscuits while Meg and Flo poured out some juice from a pink jug. Hannah, Zoe, Meg, Flo and Charly were best friends and together they made up the Glitter Girls – the coolest group of girls ever! The girls met up like this as often as they could. They took it in turns to meet in each other's bedrooms and because they all lived on the same estate, they were able to walk to see each other without having to ask for a lift from their mums and dads. The girls were all lucky enough to have their own bedrooms and they'd all had them painted the same colour, Glitter Princess, a beautiful shade of pink with a glittery shimmer on top. The Glitter Girls all loved pink and purple and anything glittery, and they were always looking out for treasures that they could use to decorate their rooms.

On this particular afternoon, it didn't take Meg long to spot the new duvet cover that Zoe had on her bed. It was pink with ballerinas twirling around all over it.

"Hey, Zoe – that's really cool! Where did you get it?" Meg asked.

"My aunt sent it to me. She found it in a shop in London," said Zoe, smiling. She had been really pleased when she'd opened the parcel.

"I love it!" said Hannah.

"Me too," agreed Flo.

"Hey, did I tell you that I'd seen some really great tights in the window of that big shop in the high street? They had these purple swirly patterns all up the legs," said Charly, taking a sip of her drink.

"Oh, I saw those," said Zoe. "Aren't they brilliant?"

"I reckon we should all save up to buy some," said Charly. "They'd go really well with our jackets, wouldn't they?"

The other girls quickly agreed. All the Glitter Girls had the most gorgeous denim jackets that Hannah's mum, who worked in a theatre as a costume designer, had customized for them.

8

They'd started off as ordinary denim jackets but Hannah's mum had embroidered "GG" on the back of each of them with pink and silver thread. She'd also made them some big pink and purple heart-shaped badges for the front of each jacket. The Glitter Girls loved the jackets and wore them whenever they could. They even wore them to school when the weather was warm enough.

"Right," said Zoe, grabbing everyone's attention. "What do we need to talk about?"

Just like they did at all their meetings, the Glitter Girls talked about what they were going to get up to next. They all liked to have something going on – like a play to write, or some jewellery to make, or a competition to enter.

"We could write a song," said Charly.

"Good idea – but who's going to write the music to go with the words?" asked Meg. Meg had a point – although all the Glitter Girls played the recorder a little, she was the only

Glitter Girl who was learning to play an instrument.

"Meg's right," said Zoe, scratching her nose. She always did that when she was thinking.

"We could write a poem instead," Charly suggested.

"Yes, but it would be nice if we could do something that might be for someone else," said Flo. "You know, not just for us."

"Well, we could give the poem to someone," Hannah said.

"Yes," said Zoe. "We could take it to the Nursing Home."

"Nice idea," Meg replied. "But what are the elderly people going to do with a poem after we've gone?"

The Glitter Girls knew what Meg meant. It wasn't really much of an idea. They sat for ages, nibbling away on biscuits and coming up with ideas for things they could do: making cards, trying out a dance routine, baking cakes, stuff like that. But there was nothing that was particularly different or that they all wanted to do. So a lot more munching and thinking went on before Zoe suddenly said, "Hey – you lot, I've got it!" She had a broad smile on her face.

"Got what?" asked Meg.

"A brilliant idea!"

"So what is it?" demanded Flo.

"Yes, don't keep it a secret!" said Hannah, who was twiddling her long red hair round her fingers.

"OK, OK! Now listen," Zoe leaned forward into the circle. All the Glitter Girls did the same as they waited eagerly for Zoe's idea. "Well . . . you know the hospital?"

"Course we do, Zoe!" said Charly impatiently, pushing her pink glasses back up her nose. "Your mum's a doctor there. Now get on with it, will you!"

"All right! Well, last night, Mum was telling me that the lady who presents the special children's programme on the hospital radio at the weekends isn't very well. So the children won't have a programme until she's better." Zoe sat back again and bit into another biscuit dramatically.

"So?" said Flo. "I mean, I'm really sorry that the lady's ill and that the children haven't got a radio programme. But what's that got to do with us?"

"Yes," agreed Meg. "It's a great shame, but we don't know any DJs."

"But can't someone else do the programme for them?" Charly asked.

"Of course they can!" said Zoe. "That's what I mean! We could help out. We could come up with some people who could do the show instead!"

"Great idea!" Meg said, grabbing a pad and pen from Zoe's desk. "I'll do a list."

The other Glitter Girls laughed. Meg loved being organized and getting the other Glitter

Girls organized too. It was so typical of her to do a list!

"I know! Mr Sampson the lollipop man would be really good. He's full of funny stories and he makes us laugh, doesn't he?" said Hannah.

"And Rachel, the lifeguard at the swimming pool! She'd be good," said Zoe.

"Yes, she's cool," Flo agreed.

"I think it would be brilliant to do a radio programme," said Hannah.

"Yes – you could play all your favourite songs," agreed Meg.

"And you could interview people," said Charly, who wanted to be a television presenter. "It would be great."

"Great? It would be *fantastic*," said Flo. "You know, I think there are some really important people that we should add to this list for Zoe's mum."

"There are?" asked Meg, chewing on the end of the pencil.

"Yes," said Charly, grinning at Flo. "Us!"

"Exactly," said Flo excitedly. "The Glitter Girls could do the programme for the hospital!"

There was a moment of stunned silence as all of the Glitter Girls thought about what Charly and Flo had said. Then suddenly, they all exploded with excitement.

"Yes!" they all cried together.

So it was agreed: the Glitter Girls were going to volunteer and Zoe was going to speak to her mum about it over the weekend. They joined hands in the circle and raised their arms victoriously above their heads, just like they always did when they had a great idea.

"Go Glitter!" they said.

Chapter 2

On Monday at school, the Glitter Girls had to wait until breaktime before they could get together to find out what Zoe's mum had said about the radio show.

"So – tell us!" pleaded Charly, as they ran into the playground.

"Yes, come on!" said the rest of them, tugging at Zoe's school sweatshirt.

"Well," said Zoe, trying to be serious. "I told Mum all about our idea and at first she wasn't very keen because she said we wouldn't be able to work all the equipment in the studio. . ."

The Glitter Girls were devastated. They'd been so excited about the idea they hadn't imagined that anything could go wrong. . .

"But," Zoe carried on dramatically, "then I reminded her that Meg's brother was really good at stuff like that and in the end she agreed to speak to the producer at the hospital!" said Zoe.

"Cool!" said Flo. "We're almost there, then!"

"But when is she going to do that?" asked Hannah.

"Yes," said Charly, "it could take ages and then we might not have very long to get ready for the show if they say yes!"

"Well. . ." Zoe peered at them sideways and grinned.

"Zoe, what have you been up to?" cried Flo.

"Well, actually, my mum's already spoken to the producer – she rang her last night – and she's agreed that we can do it!"

"You mean the programme's ours?" asked Charly.

"Yep!" Zoe was smiling from ear to ear now. "We've got to think of a name for our programme and then get together all the songs and stuff that we want to play."

"Easy peasy!" said Meg.

"Too right!" agreed Hannah. "We can put together a list of our favourite songs after school today."

"Yes – Go Glitter!" the others all agreed.

"OK, but there's one thing that you've all forgotten," said Meg, whose long wavy hair had been tied back for school with a pink hair band.

"What's that?" asked Flo.

"Oh, just the simple problem of Zoe saying that my brother will help us do it when we haven't even asked him," sighed Meg. "And he's probably playing football on Saturday."

The girls all stared at one another. Was this going to stop them before they'd even begun?

"So what are we going to do now?" wondered Hannah.

"Well, I think we'd better start with me asking Jack if he'll give us a hand. I'll probably have to promise to do something like disappear next time his girlfriend's round. Or clean the mud off his football boots! Or worse, clean out his revolting terrapins – yuck!"

"Well, if you do, we promise we'll do something to help!" said Hannah.

"Yes, we could always have a sleepover at my house if you've got to keep out of his way," said Zoe, who was feeling bad about dropping Meg in it. "And I'll do anything I can to help persuade your brother."

Meg hugged her. "I know you will. Don't worry, I'm sure I can talk him round. Now, don't we need to find a name for our programme?"

The girls thought for a while before Charly shouted, "Got it! It's obvious! Let's call the programme *Glitter FM*!"

"Brilliant!" said Hannah.

"Yes, perfect," agreed the others.

"Right," said Meg. "I'll go home after school

and suck up to my brother and you lot can go round to Charly's and start to think up the list of tracks we're going to play."

"Go Glitter!" the girls all said at once!

Chapter 3

Meg ran so fast into the playground the next morning that she almost bumped into her teacher, Miss Stanley, who was busy putting up notices about the school fête.

"Steady Meg! Goodness, you're keen to be here today," Miss Stanley said, smiling.

"Sorry Miss! I was looking for the others. Have you seen them?" Meg asked, smiling back. She didn't need to explain to Miss Stanley who the "others" were – everyone just knew about the Glitter Girls!

"They're out in the playground," Miss Stanley said.

Meg found them leaning against the wall outside their classroom. There were only five minutes left before the bell went.

"Meg! Tell us! What happened?" asked Charly.

"Yes," said Zoe anxiously. "What did your brother say?"

"Well," said Meg. "At first, he was really stroppy about it and said he had better things to do than spend his Saturday hanging around with us lot. But then I used all of my Glitter Girl charm and pointed out that he was just brilliant at working CD players and DVD machines and stuff."

"And?" Flo wanted a result!

"It didn't get him to agree straight away . . . but when I said that we'd let him speak on the programme. . ." Meg paused, teasing her friends, " . . .he said yes!"

The girls all leaped in the air at once. "Yaaay!"

Now it was Meg's turn to ask the questions.

"So, how did you lot get on with choosing some songs?" she asked.

But before anyone could answer, the bell rang and it was time to go inside, ready for the first lesson of the day.

"We'll tell you at break," Hannah whispered as they made their way inside.

★ ♥ ★ ♥ ★ ♥ ★

And that's exactly what happened. Over their snacks at break, Flo, Zoe, Charly and Hannah told Meg all about the tracks they'd chosen from their favourite bands and singers.

Meg shared in her friends' excitement – they were already well on their way to getting *Glitter FM* on air!

"Are there any of your favourites that we've missed?" said Flo.

"Don't think so. Every one you've said sounds great. What else have we got to do?" she asked.

"Well," said Zoe, fiddling with a pink butterfly clip that she was wearing in her hair, "Mum says we need to go and see the hospital radio producer on Friday after school to see if we're ready to do our first programme on Saturday!"

"What? *This* Saturday?" Flo looked as surprised as she sounded.

"Yep," Zoe smiled. "So she's going to ring round to everyone's mum tonight to see if it's OK to take us after school on Friday."

"Cool!" said Charly and Flo at the same time.

"Do you think we'll be ready by Friday?" asked Hannah. "We've got lots of other things to think about yet. You know, like what we're going to say?"

"Yes, Hannah's right," agreed Charly. "I mean, we can't just play records for a couple of hours, can we?"

"That's true," said Zoe. "Do you think we need another meeting? Tonight after school?"

"But I can't come tonight!" exclaimed Meg. "I've got my cello lesson."

"And Charly and I've got swimming lessons," said Flo.

Hannah twiddled her long ginger hair in her fingers like she always did when she was thinking. "Look, it's only Tuesday," she said. "We've got Wednesday and Thursday to talk about the programme some more."

"OK, let's meet tomorrow," said Zoe.

"You lot can come round to my place tomorrow afternoon if you want to," Flo suggested. "My sister won't be back from school until after five."

"Sounds cool to me!" said Hannah.

"Me too," said Charly, Meg and Zoe together. "Go Glitter!"

Chapter 4

Throughout the day, the Glitter Girls couldn't stop thinking about *Glitter FM*. They chatted away about it at every opportunity. Zoe was so excited about the programme that she got caught talking during assembly that afternoon and Mrs Wadhurst, the headteacher, told her off in front of the whole school! As soon as assembly was over, Miss Stanley made her go and apologize to Mrs Wadhurst.

"I'm really sorry, Mrs Wadhurst," Zoe said, looking down at her shoes.

"Well, thank you for coming to tell me, Zoe," Mrs Wadhurst smiled kindly. "I must say, you do seem to be like a jumping bean at the moment. You don't seem to be able to keep still for a moment – and I've seen you gossiping with the other girls in the playground every breaktime. What on earth are you up to?"

Zoe wasn't sure what to say. Should she tell her about *Glitter FM*? She wondered if the other girls would be cross with her if she did. But it wasn't a secret, was it? And anyway, Mrs Wadhurst was bound to find out at some stage.

"Well, you see, we're going to be on the radio on Saturday, doing our own programme. So we've only got a few days to get ready for it," Zoe explained.

"Radio programme. . .? I don't understand," Mrs Wadhurst looked puzzled.

"A radio programme . . . at the hospital," said Zoe.

"Let me see if I've got this right, Zoe. You and your friends – Meg, Charly, Hannah and Flo – are going to be on a radio programme this weekend, and it's something to do with the

26

hospital?" Mrs Wadhurst was twiddling her pen around in her fingers.

"Yes, that's right, Mrs Wadhurst. But we're not just going to be on the radio programme, we're going to be doing the whole programme ourselves. Meg's brother Jack is going to help us too. He's really good at working CD players and stuff."

"I remember Jack from when he was at this school. Yes, you're right – he was always good at IT, so I'm sure he will be really helpful at working the equipment for you, Zoe. But I don't understand *why* you're doing the programme. And how did you get to be doing it?"

So Zoe explained about the programme's normal radio presenter being ill and how the Glitter Girls had offered to help out to make Saturday afternoon in the hospital a bit more fun for the children there.

"And we're going to call the show *Glitter FM*, you see?" Zoe smiled at her headteacher.

"I do see, Zoe," said Mrs Wadhurst, remembering all the other times that the Glitter Girls had found a way to do things to help other people.

"And my mum's going to take us to see the person who runs the hospital radio station after school on Friday. And we've got to choose all our favourite hits to play before then so that we're ready," Zoe explained.

"I expect you've got other things to do as well, haven't you? Like deciding who's going to be the programme's presenter? That sort of thing," said Mrs Wadhurst, infected by Zoe's enthusiasm.

"Well actually, I think we're all going to share in the presenting of the programme," said Zoe. "We're going to meet up tomorrow afternoon after school to decide what we're going to say. We haven't had a chance to think about it yet." Zoe tucked her hands into the pockets of her school skirt.

"I shouldn't think you have," said Mrs Wadhurst. "Well Zoe, it sounds like a really exciting project you and the other Glitter Girls have got planned. And I'm sure that you will do a really good job. Now, I think it's time you got back to Miss Stanley, don't you?"

"Yes, Mrs Wadhurst." Zoe turned and opened the door. "Thank you, Mrs Wadhurst. And I'm sorry again – about talking and that in assembly."

"Yes, well, try not to do it again, Zoe. Oh, and once you've had your meeting with the others and decided what you're going to do on the programme, let me know if there is anything that the rest of us in school can do, won't you? We'll do what we can to help."

"Yes, Mrs Wadhurst, I will," said Zoe. But at that moment, she didn't have a clue what everyone could do to help the Glitter Girls with *Glitter FM*.

★ ♥ ★ ♥ ★ ♥ ★

After school, Zoe and Hannah waited in the playground for Hannah's mum. Flo and Charly had already gone to their swimming lessons and Meg was staying late after school for her cello lesson.

As they waited, Zoe told Hannah about her chat with Mrs Wadhurst. "Actually, she was quite cool about it – you know, not too stressy. Especially when I told her about *Glitter FM*. She even said that everyone at school would help us if we needed it. But what could they do?" Zoe kicked at some grit in the playground with her foot. She hated her black school shoes and wished that she could wear her trainers all the time. They had curly purple shoelaces that wound round each other and never came undone, and purple lights in the soles that made different patterns as you walked. But there was no way that Mrs Wadhurst was going to let anyone, not even the Glitter Girls, wear trainers to school, except on "No Uniform Day".

Hannah wasn't sure how everyone could help, either. "Well, maybe if we get stuck choosing songs – or if we haven't got the CDs we want. The other children could help us then, couldn't they?"

"Yes, perhaps," said Zoe, still fidgeting with her feet. "Why don't we ask the others when we meet up tomorrow? See what they think?"

"Sounds like a good idea to me," agreed Hannah. "Hey look, here's Mum."

They walked towards the car.

"Can you imagine that in only a few days we'll be on the radio?" Zoe said.

"It's good, isn't it?" Hannah replied, squeezing her friend's hand.

"It's fantastic!" Zoe squealed.

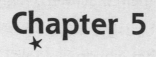

Chapter 5

Hannah and Meg knocked at Flo's bedroom door and whispered the secret password, "GG!" It was Wednesday after school and the girls were meeting up as arranged. Charly and Zoe had already arrived and when Flo opened her door to let the remaining Glitter Girls in, they were already tucking in to a huge bowl of popcorn. It wasn't long before Meg and Hannah joined them.

"So, what have we got to do today then?" asked Hannah, cramming some popcorn into her mouth as she spoke.

Meg consulted her list. "Well, we've got to finalize the playlist as well as deciding what else we're going to do on the show."

"And what's happening with Jack?" Zoe asked, looking over at Meg. She was wearing her new jeans – they were covered in sequins that formed the shape of flower petals all up her legs. The other Glitter Girls wished they had a pair too!

"Well," Meg finished munching and wiped her mouth with the back of her hand. "Actually, he's being pretty cool about it. But mostly because he says he wants a recording of the programme to use for some project he's doing at school. Something to do with his Media Studies course, whatever that is. Do you think that's OK, Zoe?"

"Oh, I'm sure it is. Anyway, we can find out on Friday when we visit the station, can't we?"

Meg nodded. "Right, let's get back to the playlist."

"I vote for *S Club 7* – all of their songs are really great!" said Charly, making patterns with her arms above her head in exactly the same way as the band did in their latest video.

"Yes, they're cool!" agreed Hannah. "And we can't do the programme without playing *Westlife*, can we?"

"Too right, we can't!" said Zoe.

"How about *Hear'Say*? They're pretty cool," said Charly.

"Their clothes are just fantastic!" said Flo, who was always trying to copy the hairstyle of one of the girls in the band.

"So, what about the other tracks we'll need? What do you think of Robbie?" Meg asked. Meg really liked him.

"Some of his tracks should definitely go on the list," agreed Hannah.

"OK then. That's cool. We've got lots of music already!" said Zoe.

"And we can watch that new chart show tonight so we can get some more ideas, can't we?" suggested Charly.

"Good idea," said Flo.

Just then, Zoe had a thought. "But how are we going to get hold of all these CDs? I mean, I've got some of them and I expect my sisters will have others. But what about you lot?" she asked.

"That's a point . . . I've only got a few CDs," said Meg.

"Well, we could ask everyone we know, couldn't we?" Hannah suggested.

"Yes! That's it! We can ask Mrs Wadhurst in school tomorrow if everyone could help us by bringing in some of their CDs," said Charly.

"Do you think she would?" Flo wondered.

"Well, yesterday she did say she'd do everything she could to help!" said Zoe. "I'll ask her if she can do something about it in assembly tomorrow, shall I?"

"Nice one, Zoe!" Charly smiled.

"Well, hopefully that's sorted, isn't it?" said Meg. "Now all we've got to do is decide what we're going to talk about."

"Yes, we can't just play music. We've got to

have something to say, haven't we?" said Hannah.

"What about stories?" wondered Charly. "We could read out the story that Zoe's sister wrote for that competition last year."

Zoe's sister, Beth, wanted to be a journalist. She'd entered a newspaper competition to write a story about a family who had survived an earthquake in India. She'd described how they had rebuilt their home and their lives after a really terrible disaster in which their grand-parents had died. Beth had won the prize for her age group in the competition and she'd been along to the newspaper in London to have her photograph taken and to collect her prize.

"Good one," agreed Zoe. "Beth would be OK about that. But we need some other stuff too."

"Yes – why don't we all look through the papers and see if we can find some other interesting stories to tell the children?" Hannah suggested.

"Yeah, there must be lots of stories about

things children have got up to – funny stuff as well as brave stuff," said Charly.

"And stories about animals, too," agreed Zoe, who desperately wanted to be a vet.

There was a knock at Flo's bedroom door.

"Hello?" said Flo. "Who is it?"

"It's Mum. Can I come in?"

"Course," said Flo, and got up to open the door.

"I just thought that you might like some of this cake that I made this afternoon." Flo's mum entered the room carrying the most delicious looking cake. It was decorated with pink fondant icing and had little silver sugar balls on the top which spelt out GLITTER FM. She put it down on the floor in the centre of the circle of girls.

"Wow!" the Glitter Girls all said at once.

"So, how are you getting on with your programme then?" Mrs Eng asked.

Of course, all their mums and dads knew

about Saturday's radio programme and it seemed like they were just as excited as the Glitter Girls themselves.

They told her what they had decided.

"Sounds like you're doing well then," Mrs Eng said, cutting the cake. "If I read any good stories, I'll let you know. I'm sure you girls could stay here all night chatting, but I think, once you've had some cake, perhaps it's time you were all getting home. It's quite late, you know. And I'm sure you've all got homework to do, too."

It was true. They all had some maths to do as well as their usual reading. And on top of that, they all had to make sure they watched the new pop-music programme on telly as well!

Chapter 6

On Thursday morning, Charly's mum took the Glitter Girls to school in the car. They weren't walking today because it was raining. Charly's sister Lily sat in the car with them and proudly showed the other girls her new doll, Treena, who was wearing a funky pair of pink dungarees.

"Glitter Girl!" Lily said, showing off her doll.

"Go Glitter!" said Meg, laughing along with Lily.

Even Lily understood how special the Glitter Girls were, and she was only three! "Go Glitter!" Lily said, giggling all over again.

The other girls were busy reporting back on the stories they'd read in the papers and watched on TV.

"Did you see that thing on the news about the little dog?" Charly asked.

"Oh, wasn't he gorgeous? He reminded me a bit of your dogs, Hannah," Meg looked at Hannah who was unpacking and repacking her ballet bag. Hannah's family had two dogs, Ruby and Opal. They were hairy in a sort of fluffy way and were quite small.

"What happened to him?" Hannah wondered out loud.

"Sorry girls," Charly's mum said as she pulled up outside school. "You'll have to find out more about the little dog later. It's time for school!"

The girls quickly gathered up their bags and coats and stepped out on to the pavement.

"Bye, Mrs Fisher! Thank you!" they all said, as Meg closed the car door.

"Bye Lily!" they waved.

"Go Glitter!" Lily waved back, still clutching Treena in her little hand.

★ ♥ ★ ♥ ★ ♥ ★

There was no time to catch up with any more news stories until breaktime. As it was still raining, the girls made the most of their break huddled in the corner of the classroom.

"So, tell us more about this dog," said Hannah to Charly and Meg.

"Well, he ran away from his owners when they were out for a walk at the beach. It was dead sad because they couldn't find him and they had to go home without him. They reported him missing to the police and everything, but after two days, no one had found him, so they thought he must be dead," said Charly.

Meg joined in. "His owners were on the television talking about it. They were really upset. But then someone was out walking and they heard barking. And it was the little dog. He was stuck down a hole!"

"They had to get the fire brigade to come and dig him out!" Charly explained. "And then he had to go to the vet's because he hadn't had anything to eat or drink for three days!"

"That poor dog!" said Flo. "Was he all right?"

"Oh yes," Meg smiled. "He was so cute! He kept barking!"

"He barked so much," said Charly, "that you couldn't hear the lady!"

"And you'll never guess what his name is! Lucky!" said Meg, before anyone could answer her.

"Sounds like he's got the right name," said Zoe. "That's a great story. Did anyone else find anything good?"

"Yes," said Flo. "My dad told me about this school that had a Book Week. It was really cool because they had a visit from an author who arrived in a really old car. The car was the star of a whole load of books that the author had written which was why he drove to the school in it! Dad said all the children from the school lined the street and waved flags when the author arrived."

"Trust you to find a story about a car, Flo!" laughed Zoe.

"Yes!" giggled Charly. "We might have guessed!"

It was a well known fact amongst the Glitter Girls – and anyone else for that matter – that the thing that Flo wanted, more than any-thing else in the world, was to be a rally driver. So Flo mentioning a story about cars was typical!

"Well it's a good story," said Hannah. "I'm sure that the children will want to hear about it on Saturday."

"Yes, exactly!" said Flo triumphantly, sticking her thumb in her mouth. Even though she was nine, Flo still sucked her thumb. She was used to people asking her what flavour it was – and she didn't care!

"What about you, Meg? Did you find anything?" asked Zoe.

"There was something in the local paper about the Donkey Sanctuary," Meg said, as she traced a raindrop falling down the outside of the classroom window.

"What about it?" asked Zoe – as usual, she was most interested in the stories that involved animals.

"They're going to have a car-boot sale to raise money so that they can look after some more donkeys," Meg replied.

The Glitter Girls went to the Donkey Sanctuary at least once every school holiday. It was one of their favourite places

"Well that's definitely something we should mention on the radio programme then, isn't it?" agreed Zoe. "We'd better find out exactly when this boot sale is so that we can tell everyone to go and help them to raise as much money as possible."

The other Glitter Girls agreed. Just at that moment the bell went. Any more talk about what was going to happen on the programme was going to have to wait until the Glitter Girls met up after school that night.

Chapter 7

At lunchtime, the Glitter Girls went to see Mrs Wadhurst and asked her if they could ask the other children for the CDs that they didn't have. Mrs Wadhurst said it wouldn't be a problem and, sure enough, she mentioned *Glitter FM* in assembly that afternoon.

"Now, children," Mrs Wadhurst said later on, in the school hall, "before you all go back to your classrooms, I've got some exciting news to tell you all. You see, the Glitter Girls are going to be making a radio programme for the children at the local hospital on Saturday afternoon!"

All the children and teachers gasped in surprise at the news!

"Yes, a proper radio programme to help cheer up all the children who've got to stay in the hospital at the weekend. But, they need your help." Mrs Wadhurst held up a piece of paper.

"This is a list of some of the CDs that the girls don't have. They were wondering if you would all be very kind and, if any of you have any of the CDs on the list, you might let the girls borrow them. You'll need to bring the CDs in tomorrow and then you can have them back on Monday. I'll put the list up on the noticeboard outside the main office. Is that OK, girls?" Mrs Wadhurst looked over at the Glitter Girls. "You just let us know if there is anything else we can do, won't you?" She looked warmly at them all and they all nodded back. Including Hannah – but she put up her hand too.

"Yes, Hannah? Is there something that you want to say?"

"Yes, please, Mrs Wadhurst. It's just that, well, I haven't spoken to the others about this yet, but I've been thinking about what we're going to say on the programme." Hannah twiddled her fingers round the heart that hung from her belt. "Anyway, I thought it would be a good idea to tell some jokes."

"I think that sounds like a very good idea Hannah," Mrs Wadhurst agreed. "And is that something we can all help you with?"

"Well, I was just wondering if everyone could write down their favourite jokes. Then we could read through them and choose the best ones to read out on the programme." Hannah carried on twiddling with her belt.

"Please, Mrs Wadhurst!" Meg's hand shot up.

"Yes, Meg?"

"I think that would be great! And then we could tell everyone at the hospital who gave us the jokes!"

The other Glitter Girls raised both hands above their heads in agreement. "Go Glitter!"

Everyone in the hall laughed.

"Well, boys and girls. I think that's sorted then. Now, there are only a couple of days before the programme. So, can all of you get organized and bring your jokes into school tomorrow? I don't want you all writing down jokes when you should be doing your school-work! OK then, everyone, when your teacher tells you, please go back to your classrooms. And remember your jokes for tomorrow!"

As all the children trooped off, they were busy chatting and already trying out their jokes on their classmates. And for once, Mrs Wadhurst didn't seem to mind!

 # Chapter 8

That afternoon, the Glitter Girls met up at Meg's house. Meg's brother, Jack, was going to be there too, so they could talk to him about the radio programme and discuss how he was going to help them with it.

"GG!" Flo and Charly knocked on the door of Meg's room.

"Come in!" Meg called. She was busy handing out drinks and doughnuts to Zoe and Hannah, who had already arrived and were sitting on Meg's bed. Both of them were wearing their Glitter Girl jackets. Hannah had her long hair tied back in a thick plait and her fringe was held off her forehead with a pink hairband. Zoe, as usual, was wearing her favourite butterfly clips in her hair.

"Doughnuts! YUM!" Flo said, tucking into hers straight away.

There was silence for a couple of seconds as the girls munched on the doughnuts. Soon their mouths were covered in sugar and they began to giggle as they all tried to lick their jammy fingers.

"I think," said Meg, "that this calls for something a bit more drastic than a few licks!" She went over to her basin and ran some water so she could wash her hands.

All of the girls loved coming to Meg's house. Each of them had a really great bedroom but Meg's was extra special – because it had a pretty, pale pink basin which sat on top of a purple cupboard. It even had a silver-framed mirror and a matching towel rail from which hung a fluffy pink towel. The soap was pink too, and had tiny shimmering specks of glitter in it!

Just as the last of them was drying their

hands, there was a knock on the door. But this time, no one said "GG".

Meg ran over to open it. "Hello? Oh, it's you Jack. Come on in. Fancy a doughnut?"

"Hi Jack," the rest of the girls chorused as he came in and sat down on the chair that Meg kept near her desk.

"Hi," said Jack, grabbing a doughnut and tucking in. It didn't take long for the doughnut to disappear. "So, what do you lot want me to do then?" asked Jack, licking the sugar and jam from his fingers.

"Well," said Zoe. "Meg's told you all about the programme on Saturday, hasn't she?"

Jack nodded.

"We've got to work out how we are going to do it all," Hannah explained. "We're going to have CDs to play, stories to read out and, we hope, some jokes from the kids at school as well."

"OK," Jack said. "So when am I going to get a

chance to speak on this programme?" He hadn't forgotten the deal he'd struck with Meg.

"Oh, I expect you'll get a chance to read out the names of some of the songs," said Charly quickly.

"What, like some of the requests?" Jack asked.

"Requests?" Zoe said. That was something that the Glitter Girls hadn't thought of before. "He's right!" she said, excitedly, "I mean, don't they normally have special messages and tracks chosen by people on radio programmes?"

"Yes!" said Meg. "But how are we going to do that? I mean, I know we're going to the hospital tomorrow, but that won't give us time to ask the children to send us requests, will it?"

"No. . ." the others all said at once. Except for Jack, who was too busy devouring another doughnut.

But then, before the others got the chance to speak, Jack said, "Why don't you find out the names of the children on the ward? I expect the doctors and nurses will let you have those. Then you could just mention their names as you go along."

"Good idea, Jack," said Charly. She thought that would be a great thing to do, especially since she wanted to be a television presenter one day. "We could find out a bit about why they're in hospital and then send them messages to make them feel better!"

"Yeah, and the children might want to send messages to each other!" said Flo. "And maybe they might want to send special notes to the doctors and nurses who are looking after them, too!"

"But how are we going to do anything about that?" said Hannah.

"I know!" said Charly. "Why don't I make up some special forms tonight? I could tell them something about the programme we're going to do on Saturday and make the bottom half of the sheet into a request form, asking them to leave it at the hospital on Saturday morning."

"Great idea!" said Zoe. "We'd have a little bit of time on Saturday morning before the programme to read through the forms and divide them up between us to read out!"

"Sorted!" agreed Charly. "I'll do some forms on my computer when I get home tonight."

"Look, you lot," Jack said impatiently. He'd finished off all of the doughnuts and had drunk two glasses of juice. "Sorry to break up the party but I've got football down at the park with my mates in a few minutes. Have you decided what you want me to do?"

"Sorry Jack," said Zoe. "We hadn't forgotten you. Mum says there's going to be someone at the hospital who will help with most of the equipment. But we need you to help put the CDs into the player, cue the tracks and make sure that the microphones are working and stuff. Does that sound OK?"

"Cool!" Jack said. "I've done the radio

programme at school a couple of times. We do one at the end of every term over the public address system. It's really wicked – the whole school listens."

"I knew you were the person to ask!" said Zoe enthusiastically. She was relieved that dropping Meg in it with her brother hadn't turned out to be too bad after all.

"Well, if that's all you need from me, I'm off," said Jack, heading for the door. "I'll see you lot on Saturday. Bye!" And he disappeared out of the door.

"Right. Now what else do we need to talk about?" asked Zoe.

Meg, organized as ever, had made each of the Glitter Girls bring their own CD cases so that they could put everything neatly away, ready to take with them tomorrow.

"Now, did you all bring your CDs?" she asked.

Immediately, all the other girls were opening up their various bags. Hannah had a little pink and green satin holdall that her mum had made her from some material that was left over from some costumes that she'd recently made. She'd embroidered it with deep pink thread and had even sewn on some tiny mirror beads. It was the perfect size for carrying CDs.

Flo and Charly both had identical pink CD cases which they'd been given for Christmas. The only way you could tell them apart was because each of them had hung their own special keyrings from the handles! Meg's CDs were simply in a pile on her bedside table, sitting next to a heart-shaped frame holding a photo of all of the Glitter Girls together on one of their outings the summer before.

"OK," said Meg, after they had sorted out the CDs they were going to take. "I think we'll have plenty if everyone at school brings in the ones on our list. Now, I've been thinking about the jokes. Why don't we just read them out in-between requests and tracks? We can just say who the joke came from and read it out."

"Excellent," said Charly. "So, I'll do the forms tonight for the requests. Is there anything else? I've got to go back and clean out my guinea pig's and rabbit's cages, or my mum will go mad! I promised to do it tonight because I forgot yesterday."

"And I've got to go back and check out some more stories my sister found for me in the newspaper," said Flo.

"Tell you what, why don't we talk about the newspaper stuff at break tomorrow?" suggested Hannah.

"OK, cool," agreed the others.

"I can't wait," said Meg, grinning from ear to ear with excitement, "Only two days to go, girls!"

Chapter 9

At break the next day, Hannah, Zoe, Charly, Flo and Meg were full of stories that they wanted to use in the programme. In the end, they chose one story each to read out on the show. Then they went to the school office to collect all of the CDs that the pupils had kindly brought in to school. There was a huge pile of jokes to collect as well! Everyone, even the teachers, had brought jokes in for them. There must have been over three hundred jokes to choose from!

The girls were so excited about going off to the hospital that evening that they found it really hard to concentrate on their lessons. But fortunately, Friday afternoons always ended with an assembly and music lesson for the whole school. It was always a great way to end the week with everyone singing together in the school hall. Mr Render, the deputy head, always took the assembly and the music lesson, and the children got to choose their favourite songs.

At the end, Mr Render told the Glitter Girls that everyone hoped that their radio programme went well, and that they wanted to hear all about it at assembly on Monday. By the time the bell went at the end of the day, the Glitter Girls could hardly control their excitement! They rushed to grab their coats and their bags and then they were off to find Zoe's mum who was waiting for them outside.

"Hello girls!" she greeted them with a smile and opened the back of the car so that they could all jump in.

"Hi, Dr Baker!" they all said in unison – except for Zoe of course, who gave her mum a quick kiss. Within seconds they were changed into their Glitter Girl jackets and T-shirts, and they were ready to go! They were so busy chatting away about the fact they were going to be real DJs that they didn't even notice the journey to the hospital.

When they got there, they followed Dr Baker along the maze of corridors until they reached the radio studio, which was tucked away in the basement of the hospital. Once they were there, they realized that *Glitter FM* really was about to happen!

Suzy, the lady who ran the hospital radio, was waiting in the studio to greet them.

"Well, hello, you lot!" she said, smiling at them. She had long blonde hair which was tied back in a high ponytail and, much to the Glitter Girls' delight, she was wearing a bright pink jumper! She even had a pair of pink satin trainers on, too!

"Hi!" the girls called back, beaming from ear to ear. They had all brought their bags containing the CDs, jokes and stories, ready to show Suzy.

Zoe's mum obviously knew Suzy really well and she quickly introduced the Glitter Girls to her, one by one.

"Well, Suzy, this little monkey is my daughter Zoe, the one who's crazy about animals. And this is Hannah – who loves dancing – and Charly – who wants to work in television – Flo – who wants to be a rally driver – and Meg – who's going to be a teacher."

"It's fantastic to meet you, girls. It's great that you are able to help us with the children's radio show – all the kids would really miss it if we had to cancel it. OK, we're going to have a busy meeting talking about tomorrow's programme and what you are going to do. You've got two whole hours to fill with music and fun!" said Suzy, as full of enthusiasm as the Glitter Girls were.

"I think, if you don't mind," said Dr Baker,

"that I will go off to check on some of my patients. Then I can leave you girls to have your meeting and come back and see you in – say, an hour's time?"

"That sounds good," said Suzy. "Now, I've got some juice in here for you girls and some flap-jacks. I thought you might be a bit hungry and thirsty after school!"

"Too right!" said Zoe.

"Yes please!" said Hannah and Charly together.

Everyone laughed.

"See you later!" Suzy called to Dr Baker, who was already on her way out of the studio.

"Bye!"

★　♥　★　♥　★　♥　★

After chatting about their choice of records and the jokes that they were going to read out, Zoe mentioned the stories that the Glitter Girls had chosen for the show.

"I'm going to read one about a little dog that got lost and was then found again!" said Meg, who was of course talking about Lucky, the dog she'd heard about on the television.

"And I'm reading out a story about Tasmin, a little girl who spent a week crushed under rubble after an earthquake, and was pulled out alive!" Hannah said.

"They both sound really excellent. What about you?" Suzy asked Flo.

"Well, I'm going to tell the children about a writer who travelled to a school in the vintage car that he writes stories about!"

"Great. The younger children will be really interested in that one. We've got a model car in the ward that the children ride in to go down to the operating theatre. It's really cool." The girls smiled. They really liked Suzy – she made them feel at ease. "Now, Zoe and Charly, what are your stories?"

"I've decided that I'm going to tell the

children all about the project that we have at our school. You see, we've got a 'twin' school in Africa and we write to the children every term and tell them all our news. We send pictures and photos too," said Zoe. "They write back to us and tell us about their lives. We have jumble sales and things like that so that we can raise money for them. Then they can buy books and paper and stuff because they don't have as much money as we do. And once a term, we all bring in a book each, so that we can send a huge parcel of books to the children as well."

"That sounds fascinating, Zoe. I'm sure the children will enjoy hearing about that. And you, Charly?"

Charly smiled. "Well, I was going to tell the children about the donkey sanctuary, but I've had another idea. I wondered if I could inter-view someone, you know – perhaps one of the nurses or doctors? Or maybe even you?" The Glitter Girls had been talking about this at lunchtime. Although Charly was keen to talk about the sanctuary, she was even more keen to interview someone again. She'd done it once for the school magazine when she'd interviewed Mrs Wadhurst. But she'd never done a "live" interview before. It was something she wanted to do in her quest to be a television presenter.

"An interview, eh?" Suzy smiled. "I'm flattered that you might want to interview me, but I will be busy in the studio with you, helping to make the programme."

"Oh," Charly slumped back in her chair, feeling disappointed.

"Tell you what, though," said Suzy. "I've got a better idea anyway. Why don't we see if we can get Mrs Teatime here for you."

"Mrs Teatime?" Charly looked as astonished as the other Glitter Girls. Surely there couldn't be anyone who was really called Mrs Teatime?

"Yes – it's a good name, isn't it?" Suzy grinned. "You see, Mrs Teatime isn't her real name, but she's called that because she's always here at teatime! Mrs Teatime comes round with the trolley in the afternoon with lots of delicious things for the children to eat and drink. Sometimes, if the children are recovering from an operation, they aren't feeling much like eating – but Mrs Teatime always manages to make them smile and find something to tempt them with! Mrs Teatime is a very special person on the children's ward."

"She sounds perfect!" said Charly, and all the other Glitter Girls agreed.

Suddenly, Charly remembered the forms she'd done for the children to make their requests. "Oh, and we've got these to hand out!" she said, and explained to Suzy how they'd thought of getting the children to write special messages for the programme.

"Well, I think that's a great idea. Tell you what, why don't I just show you how all the equipment works and explain about the headphones and the red 'on air' light," Suzy said. "Then we can pop up to the ward for you to meet some of the children and to hand out the forms."

★　♥　★　♥　★　♥　★

After leaving a note on the studio door to explain to Zoe's mum where they'd gone, Suzy and the Glitter Girls headed off upstairs to Lollipop, the children's ward. Suzy signed them all in and gave the Glitter Girls special visitors' badges.

"These young ladies," said Suzy, to the smiling receptionist behind the desk, "are going to be star DJs tomorrow on the children's pro-gramme. They're helping us out while Nancy is unwell. Aren't we lucky?"

"We certainly are!" said the receptionist, who the girls could see from her own badge was called Joanne. "So, will you girls play some music for me?" she asked.

"Course we will," said Meg. "Here, Charly's got a form for you to fill in."

Charly handed one of her forms to Joanne. "Why, thank you," she said. "When do I give it back to you?"

"We'll come back tomorrow morning and collect it from here," said Zoe.

"Yes, actually, we were wondering if you might be able to help us?" asked Hannah.

"How's that?" Joanne smiled kindly.

"Could we leave the collection box and the forms here with you?" Hannah showed the special box that she had decorated with the others at lunchtime that day. It was an old box that had once held photocopying paper. They had covered the box with pink paper and made a hole in the lid. Then they'd written GLITTER FM in glittery ink all over the sides. It looked great.

"Yep, course I will," said Joanne. "It would be a pleasure. I'll see you girls tomorrow then."

After saying goodbye to Joanne, the Glitter Girls went with Suzy to meet the nurses and doctors who were busy working on the ward. They said hello to all of the children and wrote down their names. Then they explained what the request forms were. They'd already decided that if they didn't get requests from some of the children, then they would send them a special message from the Glitter Girls anyway.

They'd just finished doing the tour of the ward when Zoe's mum appeared.

"So here you all are!" she said, looking at her watch. "I think if you've all finished, that it's time for me to take you girls home!"

"I think we've done everything we can do today," agreed Suzy, and all the girls nodded.

"Thanks, Suzy," they all said at once.

"We've had a great time," said Meg.

"Can't wait until tomorrow!" Charly beamed.

"Me neither!" agreed Hannah.

"Nor me!" Flo and Zoe said in unison.

"Go Glitter!" they all said at once!

Chapter 10

The Glitter Girls chatted all the way home from the hospital. They were so excited about *Glitter FM* that they found it hard to sleep and, sure enough, they were all up very early the next morning to get to Zoe's house for a final meeting.

Once they were satisfied that they'd got all the CDs, jokes and stories together, the Glitter Girls were ready to go. They all had their Glitter Girl jackets on, but of course, this morning, they weren't wearing their school uniforms underneath. Instead they had a selection of their very best pink, purple and glittery clothes on.

Zoe was wearing her favourite pink

dungarees. Meg had on purple and pink stripy leggings with a matching pink top. Charly was wearing jeans that were decorated with glittery braid around the bottom. Hannah wore a denim skirt that her mum had embroidered with hearts and flowers. Flo was also wearing a skirt, but hers was a purple miniskirt with a fringed hem.

"So, the Glitter Girls are going to be radio stars, are they?" said Zoe's dad, as he cleared away the breakfast things from the kitchen table with Jemma and Beth, Zoe's older sisters.

"We are!" said Charly, smiling.

"Where's Mum?" Zoe asked anxiously. "It's time to go!"

"Just behind you," said Dr Baker, pulling on her jacket. "So, are we ready?"

"Ready?" said Jemma. "They've been waiting for you to take them!"

Everyone laughed. "Well then," Dr Baker grabbed her car keys, "we'd better collect Jack and get going!"

"Bye!" the Glitter Girls called, as they trundled down the hall to the front door.

"Go Glitter!" called Beth and Jemma from the kitchen, their arms raised high in the air in support.

★ ♥ ★ ♥ ★ ♥ ★

Once they were in the hospital, the Glitter Girls could just about remember their way to the radio studio. Jack trailed along behind them, listening to his walkman.

Suzy was there to meet them.

"Well, no worries about you lot being late!" she laughed.

"No way!" said Zoe.

"This is Jack," Meg introduced her brother.

"Ah, the young man who's going to help me with the technical stuff." Suzy shook his hand.

"And I'm going to do some of the voice links as well," Jack said, determined to get what he'd come for.

"I see I have some professional competition!" Suzy smiled, making Jack feel pleased he'd let himself be dragged along to help the Glitter Girls.

"How long before we start?" Flo wanted to know. She was feeling nervous!

"About an hour, so there's plenty of time to fetch the requests down from the ward and sort through them. Then we can put the CDs in order ready to go on air!" said Suzy.

"What are we waiting for, then?" Charly said impatiently, putting down her bag.

"Yes, let's go!" agreed the others.

★　♥　★　♥　★　♥　★

After collecting the box from the Lollipop ward, Hannah, Charly and Meg read out the requests and put them in five separate piles (one for each Glitter Girl) while Flo and Zoe tried to match each request with the music. In the meantime, Suzy went through all the controls and CD machines with Jack. He seemed to know quite a lot about them already, and he explained to Suzy about the Media Studies project he'd been doing at school.

"Well, it will be a pleasure to let you have a copy of the recording, Jack. Then you can take it to school as part of your project."

"Thanks," he said.

"Now," Suzy turned to the girls, "are you lot ready for the programme?"

"Think so!" said Charly.

"When do we put our headphones on?" asked Meg.

"You've got another fifteen minutes before you are on air!" said Suzy.

"Have I got time to go to the loo first?" asked Flo.

Suzy laughed. "You have! Anyone else need to go?"

"Me!" said everyone else except Jack.

"Back here in five minutes, please!" said Suzy.

★ ♥ ★ ♥ ★ ♥ ★

Several minutes later they were in their places.

"Is everyone ready?" Suzy asked.

"Yes!" the Glitter Girls said.

"Yes!" said Jack, who was feeling very important because Suzy had put him in a seat that said *Producer* across the back.

"Ten, nine, eight, seven, six, five, four, three, two, *Glitter FM* is ON AIR!"

"Hello and welcome to the very first programme of *Glitter FM!*" said Charly, as she opened the show. "We're going to start with our first record, 'Rock DJ'. We're playing this for Jack and Suzy who are in the studio with us today."

They listened to Robbie, and then, as the record faded, the Glitter Girls introduced themselves to their audience.

"Hi, I'm Charly!"

"And I'm Meg!"

"This is Flo speaking!"

"My name's Hannah!"

"And this is Zoe. We're the Glitter Girls!"

Charly pressed the button on her microphone and spoke. "And we'd like to introduce you to Jack, Meg's brother, who's helping us today!"

"Hi dudes! Jack here!"

"And this is our jingle!" Meg looked at the Glitter Girls and, right on cue, they shouted, "Go Glitter!"

Glitter FM had begun!

★ ♥ ★ ♥ ★ ♥ ★

The first half of the programme seemed to fly by. The Glitter Girls read out the children's requests and introduced the music. Jack was brilliant at getting the CDs lined up to play right on cue.

The jokes turned out to be a brilliant way of keeping the pace of the show going and the

Glitter Girls found it hard not to laugh too much!

Halfway through the programme, Suzy read out the news headlines to the listeners. Then she got Jack to do the weather forecast.

"It may be raining outside," he said, "but the sun is certainly shining inside the hospital today with *Glitter FM*!"

Jack and the Glitter Girls were having such a great time! All the girls got the chance to read out their special stories to the children. When it was Zoe's turn, she told everyone about the twin school in Africa. Then she suggested that the children could ask their parents to bring in any books that they didn't want any more so that they could take them to school, ready to send to the African children.

By the time it was Charly's turn to interview Mrs Teatime, she was feeling very nervous. But Mrs Teatime turned out to be a lovely lady! She was so sweet that she made Charly feel like she was chatting to her next-door neighbour.

Mrs Teatime told the Glitter Girls all about her job and said, "I've been working on the Lollipop ward for ten years and I've loved every minute of it. I wouldn't change it for the world!"

"Well, thank you for joining us today, Mrs Teatime," said Charly, as she brought the interview to a close.

"It's been a pleasure. And I've got a special treat for you Glitter Girls – and Jack of course – when the programme's over."

"Thanks Mrs Teatime!" all the girls said together. Jack didn't say anything because he was busy cueing up a jingle that Suzy had in the radio record library. It was a special jingle that the DJs usually used when Mrs Teatime was doing her rounds. It was perfect!

★ ♥ ★ ♥ ★ ♥ ★

The Glitter Girls played a few more songs and read some dedications, until it was almost the end of the programme.

"It's nearly time to go now, so, on behalf of all the Glitter Girls," said Flo, "we'd like to thank Suzy, the show's producer, for helping us with the programme today."

"And we'd also like to thank Meg's brother, Jack," said Zoe, "who's helped us with the music."

"Yes," said Meg. "I hate to admit it, 'cause he's my brother, but he's been a real help!"

"We'd also like to thank everyone who has sent in requests," said Hannah. "We hope that we've mentioned all of you and played your favourite songs."

"And finally," said Charly, "we'd like to send everyone's best wishes to Nancy, who usually does the programme. We hope you feel better soon!"

"Go Glitter!" the girls called out for the last time. It was their jingle on the programme and they'd lost count of how many times they'd said it!

Then *Glitter FM* went off air with its last track

– it was the *'N Sync* song called "Bye Bye".

★　♥　★　♥　★　♥　★

As the last bars of music played, Jack and all the Glitter Girls took off their headphones and laid them down on the desks in front of them.

Suzy flicked off the ON AIR light and the girls looked at each other, beaming with pleasure. Jack was busy with the CD machines, checking that everything was turned off, and that the radio station really was off air.

"Well, girls," said Suzy, "and boy!" she laughed. "Well done! *Glitter FM* was a great programme. You should be really pleased with yourselves!"

"Wasn't it brilliant?" Charly asked no one in particular.

"It went so quickly," said Flo.

"The jokes were good, weren't they?" Hannah said.

"Especially the one about the robot and the

mummy," agreed Meg, beginning to giggle again.

Just then there was a knock at the door.

"Can I come in?" asked Zoe's mum, peering round the door. "I saw the light go off and I've got someone with me who wants to have a word with you lot!"

The Glitter Girls all looked round.

"Who?" Zoe asked.

Zoe's mum was followed in by a man who had a camera hanging from a strap around his neck.

"Hi!" the Glitter Girls called.

"What did you think, Mum?" asked Zoe. "Was it all right?"

"From what we heard, it was great," said the man with the camera.

"Oh, let me introduce you," said Dr Baker. "This is Sam. He's the press officer for the hospital. He wondered if he could talk to you and Jack about making the programme today.

He wants to take your picture as well, because he's had a word with the local paper and they might put something about *Glitter FM* in next week's issue."

"So, have you got a moment for me, then?" Sam asked.

"Go Glitter!" the girls said, punching the air. Even Jack joined in. And it was exactly that moment that Sam captured with his camera!

★ ♥ ★ ♥ ★ ♥ ★

After having their promised special treat with Mrs Teatime, the Glitter Girls were far too excited to split up and spend the afternoon on their own. So, after Zoe's mum had dropped Jack off at the park for his football match, the girls all went back to Flo's house for a good gossip.

Hanging on Flo's door was the most brilliant poster advertising *Glitter FM*. It had been painted by Flo's sister, Kim.

"That's cool!" said Hannah, who sometimes wished she had a clever older sister instead of an irritating younger brother.

In-between munching on the snacks that Flo's mum kept bringing them, the Glitter Girls went over *Glitter FM* again and again. They all agreed that it had been one of their best adventures yet. They certainly had a terrific story to tell in assembly on Monday morning!

★ ♥ ★ ♥ ★ ♥ ★

Mrs Wadhurst got the Glitter Girls to come out to the front at assembly. They told everyone what had happened, smiles beaming from their faces as they spoke.

"And did you have your own jingle, by any chance?"

The Glitter Girls knew that Mrs Wadhurst must have spoken to Suzy or someone else who had heard the programme.

"Yes!" they all said.

"Now, let me guess," said Mrs Wadhurst. "It wouldn't by any chance have been 'Go Glitter!', would it?" Mrs Wadhurst did a perfect copy of the Glitter Girls' catchphrase!

"Go Glitter!" the Glitter Girls called back.

"Go Glitter!" the whole school erupted – teachers as well!

★　♥　★　♥　★　♥　★

The local paper came out every Wednesday. As the girls charged out of school, they could see Zoe's mum standing at the school gate with the newspaper held out in front of her.

Even from a distance, the Glitter Girls could see that the picture Sam had taken of them was on the front page! They rushed over to Zoe's mum and quickly scanned the article underneath the headline "Glitter Girls sparkle over the airwaves!"

"Look what it says!" said Charly, bursting with excitement.

"After such a successful programme," read Meg, "Suzy Jenkins, the producer of the hospital radio station, is going to ask the Glitter Girls to come back and present further *Glitter FM* shows until the programme's usual presenter is well enough to return."

"She is?" shouted Hannah.

"Brilliant!" said Flo.

"Go Glitter!" said Zoe.

"Go Glitter!" the others replied.

★　♥　★　♥　★　♥　★

So that was how *Glitter FM* was launched. After four weeks, Nancy was better, and she returned to make the children's programmes for the hospital radio station. But whenever she or Suzy needed any help, the first people they called on were the Glitter Girls, who were always happy to be DJs again for a while, on their very own *Glitter FM*.

Don't miss:

Magical Makeovers

It was Friday afternoon, and Hannah, Flo, Meg, Charly and Zoe – best known to everyone as the Glitter Girls – had just finished school, and were walking towards Zoe's mum's car. Zoe's mum, Dr Baker, was taking them home.

"So, what are we going to do?" asked Meg, tucking a stray piece of her long, wavy blonde hair behind her ear. She was lugging her cello along as well as struggling with her book bag.

Friday afternoons were music afternoons at the girls' school and, today, Meg and the other children who played instruments had been asked to bring them along to make up an orchestra.

"Whatever we do, it's got to be great!" said Hannah enthusiastically.

"Course it has! But what are we going to do?" Charly said impatiently.

"Do about what?" Dr Baker asked, opening the back door of her car.

"The school fête. Mrs Wadhurst asked all of us at assembly to think of what stalls we could run at the fête," said Flo, climbing into the car behind Zoe.

"The school fête already?" said Dr Baker in disbelief. "It only seems like yesterday that you girls were running the tombola stall at the last fête."

"Well, the tombola stall is going to be done by some of the boys this year," Meg said, piling into the car behind the others.

"And anyway," muttered Hannah, bending over balletically to pick up her book bag, which she'd dropped, "we've got to do something different, haven't we?"

"But what?" moaned Zoe. "Some of the other girls are doing a craft stall. And Mrs Wilmott is going to run the donkey and pony rides with her daughter and the people from the Donkey Sanctuary."

"I'm sure you'll think of something," smiled Dr Baker, driving away from school. "You Glitter Girls always have great ideas, don't you? So I'm certain you'll be doing something really terrific at the fête."

The journey home wasn't far and the Glitter Girls chatted away about the other stalls that their friends were going to be running. But none of them could think of an idea for something new.

"Right," said Zoe, "I've got to hurry up and get changed for my riding lesson. But I'll see you lot at Charly's house tomorrow morning – we can talk more then."

Hannah grabbed her book bag and jumped down from the car. "I've got to rush too – my girls! Thanks Dr Baker!" And she was off down the road to her house.

"Bye!" the others called.

"So we'll meet up at my house tomorrow at nine, then?" Charly said to Flo and Meg.

"You bet! I can't wait to see Girl's Dream," said Flo.

Girl's Dream was a new shop that had opened at the big shopping centre just outside town. The Glitter Girls had read about it in the paper and it sounded fantastic! The article had said that the shop had all sorts of things that girls would love: hair accessories, make-up, clothes, bags, pens and pencils – everything that girls could dream of!

"I'd better rush too – there's my dad!" said Meg. "See you all tomorrow! Bye Dr Baker!"

Meg and her older brother and sister didn't live with their dad and this afternoon he was collecting them from home to take them out to tea.

"Bye Meg!" said Charly and Flo, who were the only two left.

"Come on, let's go. Mum says she's going to let us have pizza for tea!" said Charly.

"My favourite!" said Flo, and she followed Charly to her house, more than happy to eat pizza while she waited for her mum and dad to get home from work.